MR. FUZZBUSTER
Knows He's the
FAVORITE

by Stacy McAnulty ★ illustrated by Edward Hemingway

two lions

Text copyright © 2017 by Stacy McAnulty
Illustrations copyright © 2017 by Edward Hemingway

Published by Two Lions, New York

www.apub.com

Amazon, the Amazon logo, and Two Lions are trademarks of Amazon.com, Inc., or its affiliates.

ISBN-13: 9781503948389 (hardcover)
ISBN-10: 1503948382 (hardcover)

The illustrations are rendered in pencil, ink, and digital media.

Book design by Sara Gillingham Studio
Printed in China

First Edition

10 9 8 7 6 5 4 3 2 1

To my mom, Joanne Southwell.
Love, your favorite!—S.M.

For Takota Levi Neumann and
Stella Lockwood Neumann—E.H.

Mr. Fuzzbuster knew he was
Lily's favorite.

They'd been together since he fit
in a teacup and she fit in diapers.

They did everything together.

Naps.

 Arts and crafts.

Story time.

Dress up.

Walks.

Meals.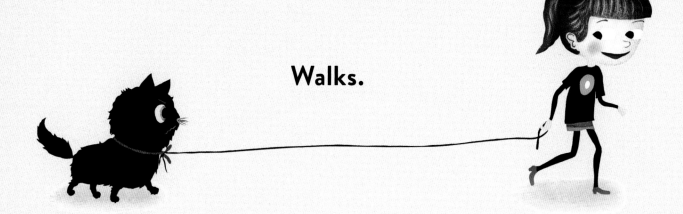

 And more naps.

But now four more animals
lived in the house.
And they had other ideas.

"I'm her favorite,"
bubbled
Fishy Face.

"No, it is I
who am the favorite,"

hissed King.

"Bless your heart, I'm that sweet girl's favorite,"

squawked Feathers.

"Favorite, Favorite! Favorite,"

barked Bruiser.

"My dear roommates,"
Mr. Fuzzbuster interrupted.
"Perhaps you forgot the official document."

The picture was old, slightly torn, and
smelled funny, but it was still absolutely true.

And Mr. Fuzzbuster was going to prove it.

In his best paw writing,
he wrote a note.

When Lily read it, she giggled.
"This is an easy question."

Mr. Fuzzbuster purred.
Yes, easy and quick.

But Lily walked past him.
What?!?

"Hi, Fishy Face," Lily said.
The fish swam in dizzying circles.

Mr. Fuzzbuster could swim like that too.
If swimming didn't involve getting wet.

"Fishy Face, you are my favorite . . ."

"... goldfish."

Mr. Fuzzbuster smiled secretly.
Of course Fishy Face wasn't *the* favorite.

But being the oldest and wisest, Mr. Fuzzbuster knew it was his responsibility to make the goldfish feel better. "Cheer up. You may not be the favorite, but you're as quiet as a cat. That's why I have not once considered eating you. And I'm a big fan of seafood."

Lily walked past
Mr. Fuzzbuster again.

"H-ello,"
Feathers squawked.

Mr. Fuzzbuster could
squawk if he wanted to.

"Feathers," Lily said,
"you are my favorite . . ."

"... bird."

Mr. Fuzzbuster felt sorry for the bird.

"There, there, Feathers. You sing
almost as nicely as I yowl,
and you're a fine roommate.
That's why I have not once
considered eating you."

Then Lily went to King's tank.

"Greetings, Your Highness." She curtsied.
"May I offer you some bugs for a snack?"

Mr. Fuzzbuster would eat a bug, but only for Lily.

"King, you are my favorite . . ."

"... lizard."

Mr. Fuzzbuster patted King with his paw.
"Poor King. Don't take it too hard.
You climb almost as well as a cat.
And I've never ever ever, not even once,
thought about eating you."

Just one more to go before Lily told them
he was her favorite. Mr. Fuzzbuster
didn't mind waiting. Everyone knew
you always save the best for last . . .

"Where are you,
Mr. Fuzzbuster?"
Lily called.
"Where's my kitty?"

"There you are,
Mr. Fuzzbuster.
You are my favorite . . ."

It was him.
He was the favorite.
Lily's favorite!
He knew it!

"... cat."

That meant . . .

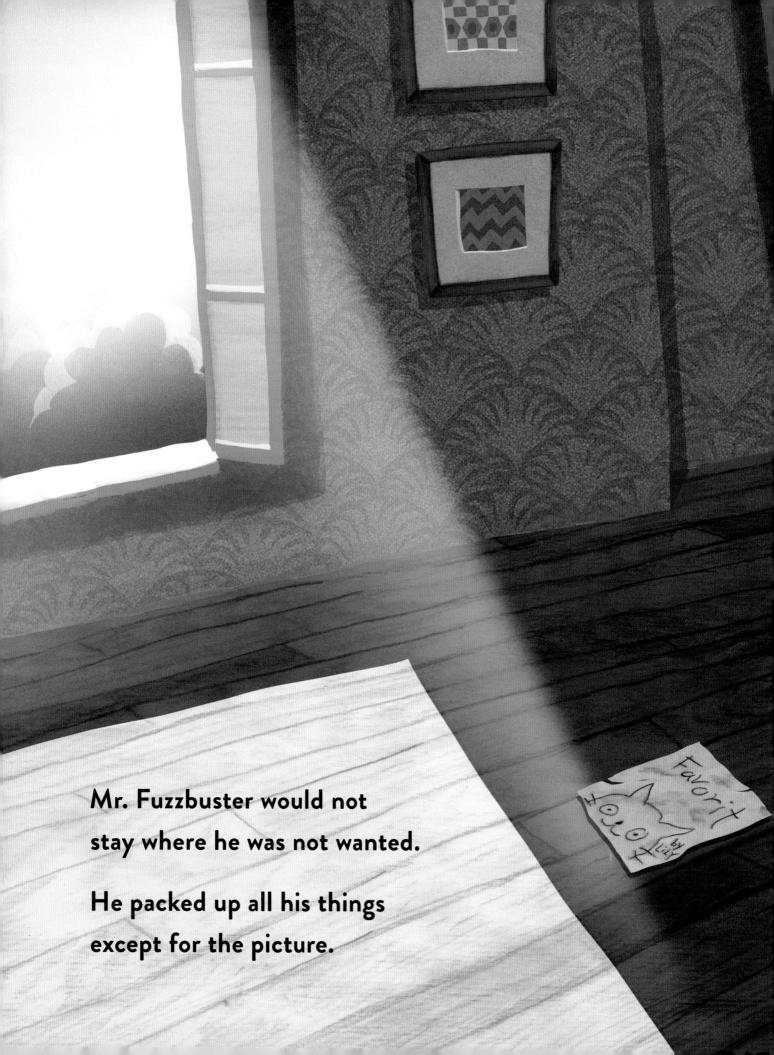

Mr. Fuzzbuster would not
stay where he was not wanted.

He packed up all his things
except for the picture.

He was almost out the
door when he heard Lily.

"Bruiser," she said, "you are
my favorite . . ."

"... doggy."

Huh?!
Not Fishy Face.
Not Feathers.
Not King.
Not Bruiser.
Not him.

It didn't make sense.
She had to have a favorite.

Mr. Fuzzbuster had a favorite.

His favorite was the one he reminded to open his cans of food.

MEOW

The one he encouraged to pet his belly by purring loudly.

Purrrr

The one who always lost when
they played catch-the-string.

And the one who said she had a favorite goldfish, bird, lizard, dog, and cat.

Mr. Fuzzbuster shredded the first note he'd written to Lily about favorites.

Then he wrote a new one.

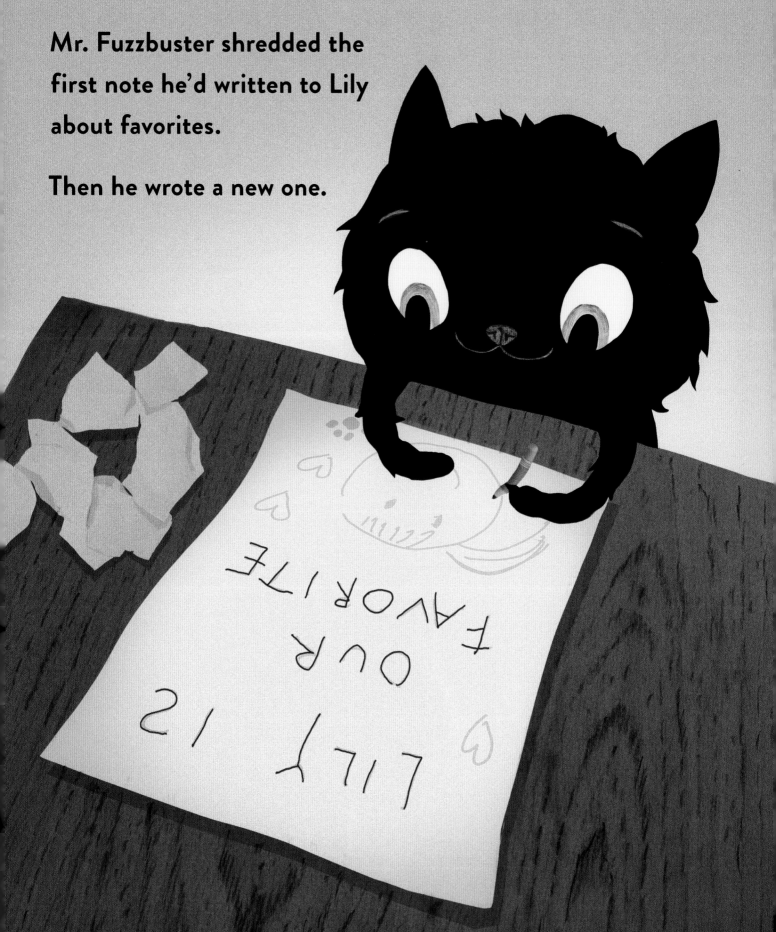

They all agreed.

"Good night, my favorite goldfish."

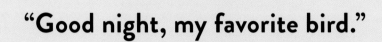

"Good night, my favorite bird."

"Good night, my favorite lizard."

"Good night, my favorite dog."

"Good night, Mr. Fuzzbuster—

my favorite cat."

Then Lily crawled into bed
and hugged her doll.

"And good night, CoraBelle." Lily yawned.
"My favorite . . ."